ARTURO
The King of the Trapeze

TINA
The Tightrope Walker

THE PARASITE PYRAMID with
SARAFLEANA at the tippy-top

Z Z Z Z Z Z Z Z Z Z Z Z

THE FLEAT

Practice area

The Fleatastics' village

Flea maternity hospital

"The Tail End" retirement home

BOYDS MILLS PRESS
AN IMPRINT OF HIGHLIGHTS
Honesdale, Pennsylvania

ASTICS

THE GREATEST SHOW ON DOGS!

Snoozer sleeps
22 hours a day.

LISA DESIMINI

She loves dogs!

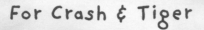
For Crash & Tiger

Boyds Mills Press
An Imprint of Highlights
815 Church Street
Honesdale, Pennsylvania 18431
Printed in China

ISBN: 978-1-62979-303-0
Library of Congress Control Number: 2016942362

Design by Barbara Grzeslo
Production by Sue Cole
First edition
The text of this book is set in Weiss.
The illustrations were created using
paper collage, paint, and a computer.
10 9 8 7 6 5 4 3 2 1

WELCOME
to
SLEEPY OLD
SNOOZER
~
Home of
The Fleatastics

Bring them back
for checkups when
they hatch.

Wheeeeeeeee!

I'm allergic to something.

I can tell it's a nice day!

We hatch in one to twelve days.

You're crowding me.

Shhhh!

Why did the egg cross the road?

You're cracking me up!

Sarafleana was a born jumper.

The older she got,
the more she jumped.

She leaped in the morning,

bounded in the afternoon,

and sprang up at night.

Her brothers and sisters liked to climb.

They liked to balance.

They liked to build.

As Mom and Dad watched their acrobatic children, they made a plan.

When Sarafleana and her siblings were old enough, the family auditioned for the famous acrobatic troupe, The Fleatastics. Even though Sarafleana couldn't stay still, the troupe's leader, Mr. Itchy, signed them up.

Sarafleana's family expected high-flying Sarafleana
to be happy at the tippy-top of their Parasite Pyramid.
But Sarafleana couldn't stop jumping.

She wanted to be applauded for her jumping ability, not scolded
for it. What if she could earn her own act in The Fleatastics?
She could be SARAFLEANA, THE HIGHEST-JUMPING FLEA EVER!

Every night, after the fleas of Snoozer
were tucked into their beds,
Sarafleana practiced.

One morning, Mr. Itchy and The Fleatastics packed up and parachuted to Sparky, a nearby sleeping dog. It would be her family's first time performing with The Fleatastics, and Sarafleana was going to prove to everyone that she deserved her own act.

As the crew set up,
Sarafleana secretly practiced.

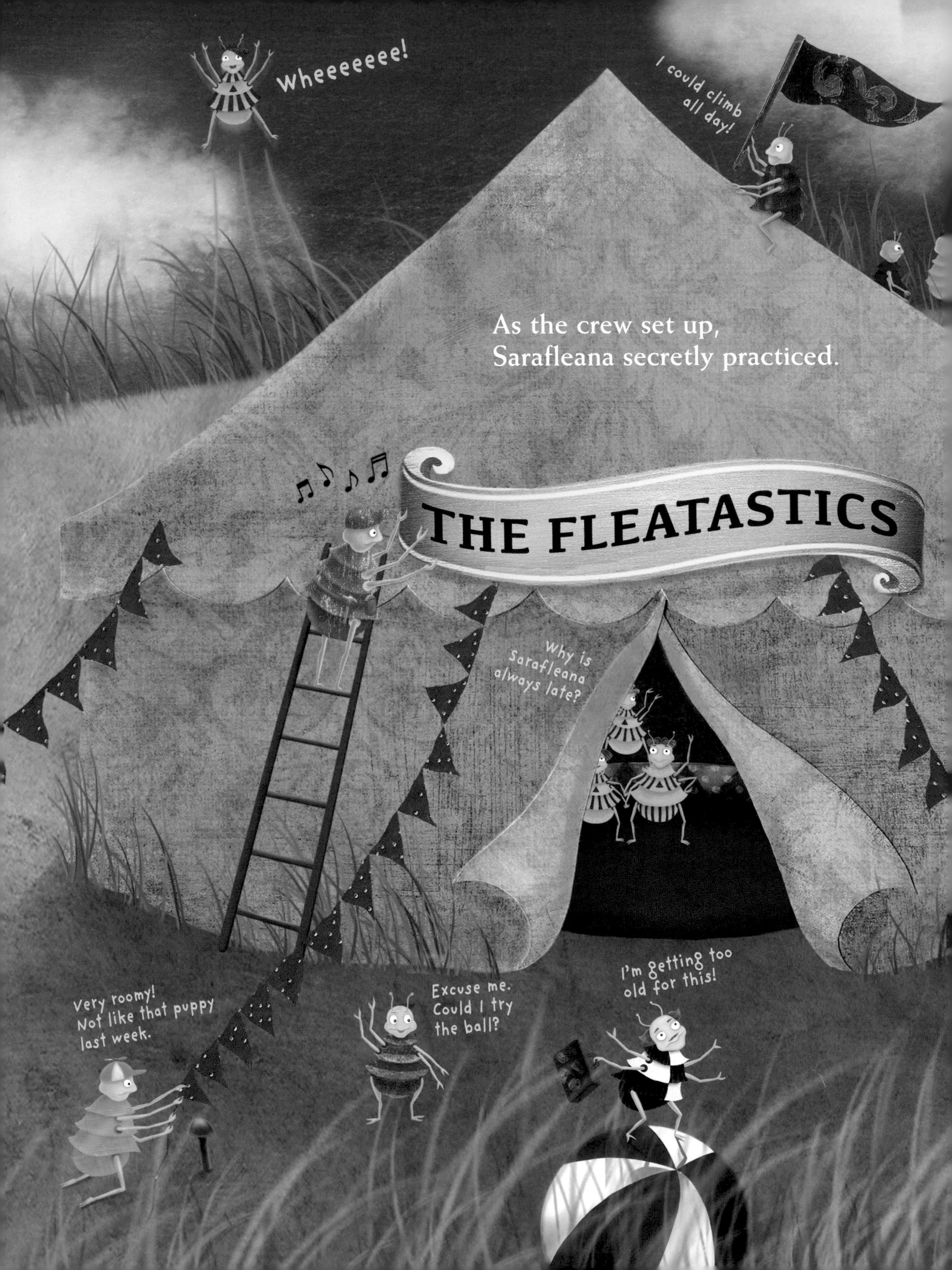

WELCOME TO THE FLEATASTICS! THE GREATEST SHOW ON DOGS!

Gregor rolled 'round.

Connie contorted.

Tina tip-toed.

Holly spun her hoops.

And Sarafleana watched longingly.

Finally, it was time for the Parasite Pyramid. Sarafleana climbed to the top. She bent her knees. She was about to prove that she was the highest-jumping flea ever. But she couldn't leap— not even a tiny bit! What were her brothers doing?

Sarafleana couldn't watch the rest of the show.
She didn't look up until the grand fleanale.
Then, seeing Arturo swinging,
Sarafleana knew she had to try again.

SUDDENLY . . .

I want another TREAT!

GASP

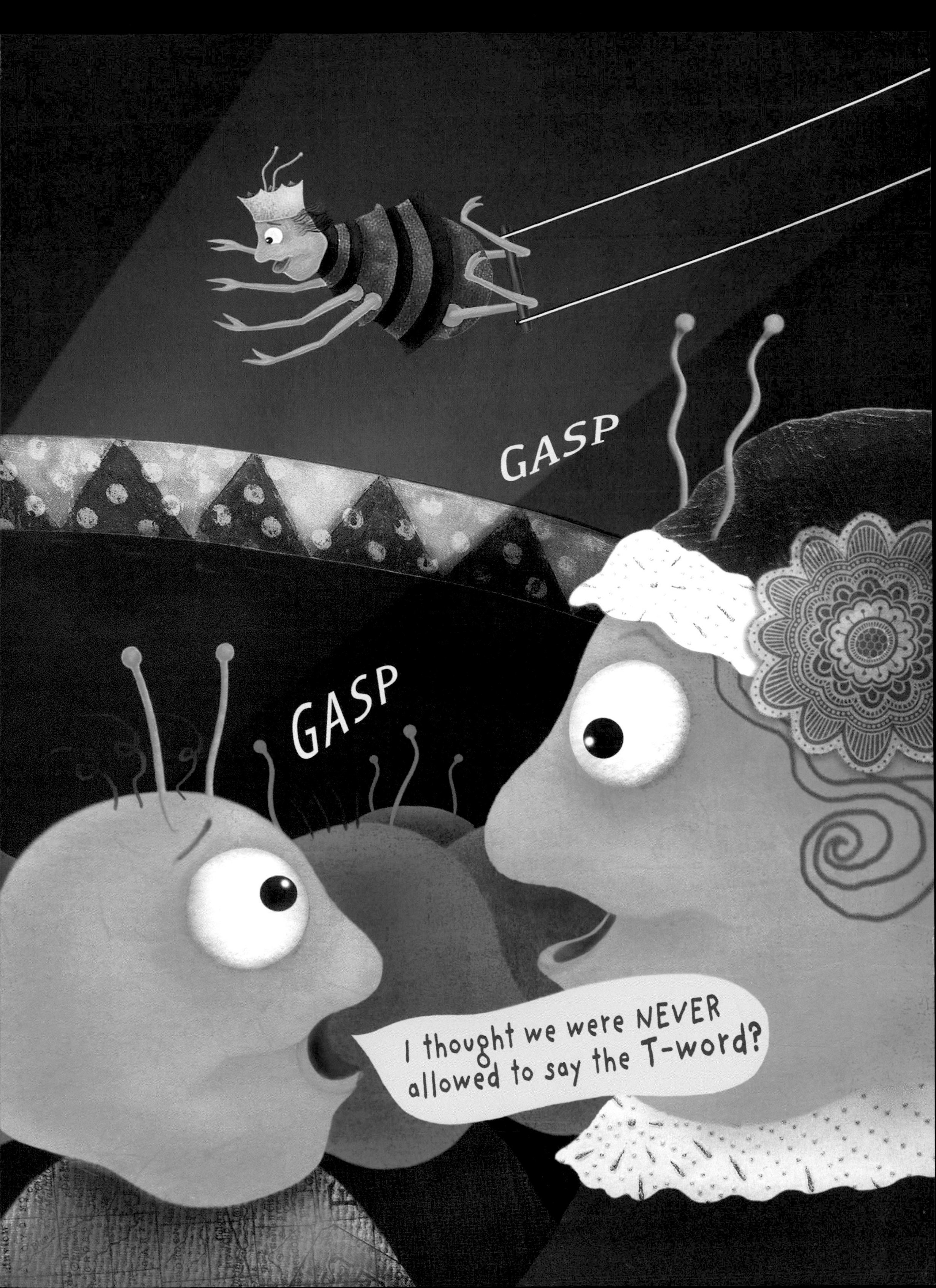
GASP
GASP
I thought we were NEVER allowed to say the T-word?

The tent bucked up and down, and a big nose poked in. "GET BACK!" shouted Sydney, the dog tamer.

THAT NOSE! Sarafleana had an idea. Her timing would need to be perfect. She leaped . . .

The dog started to scratch and scratch.
Sarafleana saw Sparky's bobbing tail and
had an inspiration. Could she jump
farther than ever before?

Even though the tail was moving, she managed to land and—carefully, bouncily—stand. It had been her best jump ever, but she wasn't done yet. Immediately she began shouting again.

The dog ran in circles and the fleas fled.

Connie is more fleet-footed this way.
I wish I had two extra legs!
I could run faster on a tightrope.

One by one, they slid down Sparky's ear,
and with another enormous leap,
Sarafleana joined them.

These days, Sarafleana has her very own act—
SARAFLEANA, THE HIGHEST-JUMPING FLEA EVER.

She's always ready if anyone accidentally says
the T-word.

But she's happiest simply springing high,
wind in her antennae, listening to the music
of the applause below.

APPLAUSE!

APPLAUSE!

I want to be just like Sarafleana
when I grow up!

BRAVA!

WE'RE HOPPING TO SEE YOU AGAIN SOON!

MR. ITCHY
The Master of Ceremonies

TINA
The Tightrope Walker

CONNIE
The Contortionist

BILLY
The Ball Roller

HOLLY
The Hoop Spinner